The Adventures of Buttercup and Granny

by

Raquel Solomon

To order additional copies of this book, contact:
Xlibris
844-714-8691
www.Xlibris.com
Orders@Xlibris.com

ISBN: Softcover   978-1-6641-2922-1
         EBook   978-1-6641-2923-8

Print information available on the last page

Rev. date: 09/15/2020

The Adventures of Buttercup and Granny

Dedication

This book is dedicated to Jermarie's Paw Paw, Eugene Lamar Lothridge. We were blessed that he was able to see a draft copy of this book before his passing and was so excited about the publishing of this book.

We will continue to keep him in our hearts and our stories as we have so many more memories of him to share with you.

We love and miss you every single day daddy.

Hi friends my name is Jermarie Pierre Johnson, Jr. but my Granny calls me Buttercup

I like spending the night with Granny and jumping on her bed. Granny's house is so much fun because we laugh a lot and eat cupcakes.

Granny loves to take me to get ice cream and pizza.

My granny takes me fun places like the mall.

She always buys me a sweet treat.

I have a dog named Lilo.

Lilo is super fun to play with and
she likes French fries too

This is my Auntie Maddy she's super fun!

I had a grandpa that I called Paw Paw he is in Heaven. He was the best Paw Paw ever!

I have another Granny and I call her Real Granny and she gives me lots of hugs and kisses.

This is my super pretty mom, Taylor. Grown ups call her Bolo. But my Granny calls her Tink.

Meet my dad we have the same name.

"Jermarie Pierre Johnson"

I call him Dad and he calls me 3J.

Thank you for reading all about me
and my Granny's fun adventures!
Stay tune for more fun.

Follow us at @StinkyandGranny on Instagram